More Than Words

Caroline's failed marriage wasn't her fault--the blame for that falls squarely on her neglectful, cheating husband--but she still has to deal with the fall-out, including her embarrassed family and all the men who now think she's hot-to-trot. When the offer of a beach vacation comes her way, she jumps at it: two weeks by herself in the sun and sand is just what she needs.

Meeting a handsome soldier who's about to go overseas isn't in her plans, but Caroline is drawn to Tom as soon as she sees him. In his arms, she learns more about passion than she could ever imagine. Just one night with him will change her forever.

This is a work of fiction. Similarities to real people, places, or events are entirely coincidental.

MORE THAN WORDS
First edition. February 2, 2015.

Copyright © 2015 Emma Fallon
Written by Emma Fallon
Cover by Olivia Hardin

ISBN: 978-1-68230-409-9

All rights reserved. Without limiting the rights under copyright reserved above, no part of this publication may be reproduced, stored in or introduced into retrieval system, or transmitted, in any form, or by any means (electronic, mechanical, photocopying, recording, or otherwise) without the prior written permission of both the copyright owner and the above publisher of this book.

This is a work of fiction. Names, characters, places, brands, media, and incidents are either the products of the author's imagination or are used fictitiously. The author acknowledges the trademarked status and trademark owners of various products referenced in this work of fiction, which have been used without permission. The publication/use of these trademarks is not authorized, associated with, or sponsored by the trademark owners.

This book is licensed for your personal enjoyment only. This book may not be re-sold or given away to other people. If you would like to share this book with another person, please purchase an additional copy for each recipient. If you're reading this book and did not purchase it, or it was not purchased for your use only, then please return to your favorite book retailer and purchase your own copy. Thank you for respecting the hard work of this author.

more than words
an erotic short story
Emma D. Fallon

All in all, it wasn't a bad trade: two weeks at my aunt's beach house in Ocean City, New Jersey in the middle of June, in exchange for not attending my cousin Lorraine's wedding. I hadn't planned to be there anyway, but if Aunt Susan felt that keeping the family divorcee—that was me—away from her precious daughter's perfect day was worth prime weeks at the shore, who was I to argue? It was the perfect time to be here, when the days were long and perfect and the nights were still chilly enough to need a sweater on the boardwalk.

I stared out over the ocean, pretending I was the only girl on the sand. It was hard to do it, when a bunch of little kids were screaming on the blanket next to me. I slid a glance in their direction without turning my head. Three small girls dug shovels into the sand, chattering away, while two boys chased each other, shouting. Their mothers sat on webbed beach chairs, wide hats on their heads, cigarettes in hand.

From behind my sunglasses, I watched them. Both of the women wore the same type of bathing suit, one-piece, shirred up the front with material that stretched nearly to mid-thigh. Broad straps crossed the shoulders. They were both around my age, but all resemblance ended there: the sun glinted off gold bands on their left hands, while my hand was bare, with only the faintest trace of a tan line. Plus, my never-had-kids body was in a bikini and looked damn good.

Or so the man lounging on the blanket on my other side seemed to think. His wife sat next to him, absorbed in her copy of *Life* magazine, and their two children were playing in the surf. But Mr. Family Man wasn't shy about how his eyes roamed over me. He started at my legs, already tanned, and moved up to what he could see of my ass. He lingered on my flat stomach and then leered at my boobs. I glared, hoping he'd get the message, but he only smiled bigger. I looked away. What a dick.

It was 1965, for the love of Mike. But as enlightened as we thought we were, being divorced put me square in limbo-land when it came to men. The young men who were tossing around a football near the water were probably about my age, but to them, I'd only be a one-night stand at best. They were more interested the sorority chicks giggling on the blanket and watching them show off, innocent young girls who still believed in the promise of happily-ever-after. That wasn't me.

On the other hand, Aunt Susan's next-door neighbor had looked at me this morning the same way the married jerk here on the beach did. He was a balding man easily twice my age, with a paunch and a double chin. This morning he'd been trimming the hedge when I'd loaded the car for the beach.

"You must be Susan's niece." The words were simple enough, but the knowing smirk made my skin crawl. Nevertheless, I forced a smile.

"Yes, I am. I'm Caroline Rogers." I hated that I still had that name as a reminder of two wasted years with James, but my parents had pitched a fit when I'd brought up taking back my maiden name.

The man came toward me, holding the oversized clippers in one hand as he extended the other toward me. "George Simpson. Susan told us you were going to be down for a few weeks."

I nodded. "You live here year-around?"

"Nah, just summers. The wife and I live in Philly during the winter." His eyes dropped to my shoulders and then to my breasts. They were hidden beneath the bright orange cover-up I wore over my bathing suit, but I could almost feel him imagining their shape and size. I folded my arms across my chest, and Mr. Simpson licked his lips.

"You know, the wife plays bridge with the old biddies up the block. Every Tuesday night. I'm home by myself for the whole evening. . .if you should get lonely and need some company."

I dropped my beach bag into the backseat of the convertible. "Thanks. I don't get lonely. I like being by myself."

"Aw, come on." He took another step toward me. "I know what it's like with women who were married and then aren't anymore. You got needs. I'm only trying to help."

I gritted my teeth. "The only needs I have, Mr. Simpson, are to be left alone and not bothered by anyone." I swung open my car door. "And if you don't get that, I'd be happy to tell your wife about your invitation. You know, I'm sure she'd be proud of what a good neighbor you're trying to be."

His face twisted into a scowl, and his eyes narrowed. I slammed the door and started up my engine, careful to keep my eyes on the road as I backed out of the driveway.

Sitting with my feet in the hot sand now, I sighed. Avoiding the bastard next door was going to make the next two weeks challenging, but I'd deal. I might have been only twenty-five, but I'd had my share of fending off men who thought what I needed was between their legs. Those guys seemed to think that a girl with a nice rack and a curvy ass was an open invitation to a good time. Even when I was married, I'd had more than my share of propositions. I never thought twice about turning them down. Nice girls didn't screw around on their husbands.

Husbands, on the other hand, apparently were okay to screw around on their nice-girl wives.

Damn it, I was over that. No more thinking about James and what might have been. That chapter of my life was over, and the book was shut. Re-reading it wasn't going to change a thing, and besides, the divorce had been the best thing that could've ever happened to me. I was free now, independent of James. And after this vacation, I was going home to tell my parents that I was moving out. I'd find a job, get my own apartment, and I'd start to live, for real this time. No more stupid fairy-tale-happily-ever-after crap. I lay back on the blanket, closed my eyes and drifted off, letting the warm sun lull me into a doze.

By the time I opened my eyes, the shadows were lengthening, and most of the groups around me were packing to leave. I stood up and stretched, and then wandered down to the ocean again, letting the cold water rinse off my sandy feet. Listening to the laughter and chatter of the families around me, I was suddenly reluctant to go back to Aunt Susan's house, with the evening alone looming in front of me.

I liked to be alone, I reminded myself. It was what I wished for every night as my parents settled into the living room with the television set blaring, talking to each other about meaningless nonsense until I wanted to scream. If I hid in my room, they accused me of being anti-social. But some nights, the monotony of their lives was too much to take, and I had to retreat or explode. So I should've been leaping for joy at the idea of peace and solitude.

But an odd sort of restlessness had taken hold of me. I'd learned during my brief marriage that I could be lonely even in a room full of people, and I could feel satisfied with only my own company. At this moment, however, I craved the touch of another human being with a tangible ache. I wanted someone to laugh with me, to look into my eyes and know what I was thinking even before I voiced the words.

I folded my blanket, stuffed it into the wicker bag along with my towel and pulled my bright orange and yellow cover-up over my head. My feet were still covered with sand, so I carried my sandals as I made my way over the dunes to the sidewalk. The cement was hot, and I hopped from one foot to the other as I struggled to brush off the sand and put on my shoes.

As I rounded the corner, I stopped short. A tall man dressed in soldier's khakis stood next to my car, leaning on the hood. I was rooted to the ground and was nearly run over by the woman walking behind me. As it was, she smacked her beach chair into the back of my legs.

"Ow!" I spun to glare at her.

"You don't just stop in the middle of the sidewalk. I could've knocked you down. You're lucky I didn't."

The soldier had turned to look at us, and when the beach-chair lady pushed past me in a huff, his eyes stayed on me. I took a few steps forward, reached my car and dropped the beach bag on the floor of the backseat.

"Can I help you?"

He didn't drop his gaze from my face. "This is your car?"

"Yep." I patted the boot. "A well-earned reward for surviving two years of hell."

He cocked his head, one side of his mouth turning up in a puzzled smile.

I waved my hand. "Never mind. Private joke. Did you need something?"

"No. I was just admiring her. I had a 64 ½. Sold her when I signed up." He ran his fingertips across the top of the door. "Mine was candy apple red, though. I like the powder blue. That would've been my second choice."

"Why'd you sell it? Couldn't you just have had your family hold on to it until you got home?" I leaned against the back of the car. There was something about this man—some kind of wistfulness that caught at my heart. His eyes were bright blue, and there was regret in them as he looked down at the Mustang again.

"I didn't want to bother anyone. Most of my friends live in apartments without garages." The fact that he referenced his friends and ignored my mention of family didn't escape me. We were both silent for a minute, and then I took a deep breath.

"Do you want to take her for a spin? You know, for old times?"

His eyes flashed up at me, wide with surprise. "Are you—gee, really? I mean, you don't have to do that. You don't know me. You probably have some place to go."

I laughed. "Not hardly. Here you go." I reached down into the side pocket of the beach bag, retrieved the keys and tossed them to him. "Think fast."

He caught them easily and held the ring on one finger, staring at the keys as though they were something rare and precious. I moved toward the front passenger side and wrapped my fingers around the handle.

"No, let me." He stepped closer, and I breathed in the tantalizing aroma of soap and some kind of light cologne. He closed his hand on top of mine. The touch of his skin sent a buzz up my arm, but I didn't move as he squeezed, his thumb pushing the button that unlatched the door.

I slid into the seat, and the soldier closed the door behind me. He picked up the small duffel that had been on the ground at his feet and made it around the back of the car in a few strides. He hesitated only a minute before he dropped the bag into the back and climbed into the driver's seat. But he didn't put the keys in the ignition right away. Instead he turned toward me and stuck out his right hand.

"If I'm going to drive your car, I should probably introduce myself." The tip of his tongue came out and touched the side of his mouth. "I'm Tom Lawson."

I stared at his hand and then laid mine within it. "Caroline Rogers."

Tom's eyes flickered to my other hand, to the bare finger. "Nice to meet you, Miss—"

"Just call me Caroline."

He nodded. "Caroline, then. Listen, are you sure you want to do this?"

I raised one eyebrow. "Let you drive my car? Yeah, I'm sure." I touched his arm. "It's the least I can do for one of our boys in. . .khaki."

His lips twisted into a smile that didn't have any humor or warmth. "Right." He turned the key, and the smile became real as the engine roared to life.

We rode down the block, heading north toward the boardwalk. I watched Tom's hands on the hard plastic of the steering wheel, caressing the ridges with long fingers.

"Do you know where you're going?" I glanced at the houses as we passed. "Are you from here?"

He shook his head. "Not from here, but I used to come down when I was a kid." He paused, as though making up his mind whether or not to say more. "I lived outside Princeton until I was fourteen. Then my parents died, and I had to move to California with my aunt. I haven't been here for fifteen years."

"I'm sorry." The words came automatically. "Okay, turn left here."

He did as I suggested without question, but force of habit made me apologize. "I didn't mean to sound like I was telling you what to do."

Tom grinned. "You didn't, but why wouldn't you? I just said I'm not from this area. I want you to tell me the best route. To wherever it is we're going."

I shrugged. "My experience has been that men don't like to be told what to do. Even when women are the ones with the answers."

"I don't know what kind of men you've been around, but any guy who gets bent out of shape when a girl speaks up is a dipstick."

Warmth flooded my chest. "Do you listen to your girlfriend? Or your wife?" He wasn't wearing a ring, but some men didn't. James certainly hadn't.

"I don't have either, but if I did, yeah, I'd listen to her."

A smile stretched my lips. "You must have had. . ." I stretched my memory back to the freshman psych class I'd taken, trying to remember what the term was. "Positive female role models."

"My mom was the smartest person I ever knew, and my aunt's a lawyer. She would have beat me if I ever said she didn't know what she was talking about."

"A lawyer?" I couldn't help the envy in my voice. "That's what I wanted to be. Oh, take this right."

"Where are we going?" Tom sped up and put the car into third gear.

I closed my eyes and let the wind blow my hair back. "Margate. It's a nice ride."

"Okay." We picked up more speed. "So why didn't you become a lawyer?"

"Excuse me?" I opened one eye to look at him. "Oh. My father didn't feel it was a good option for me. Because, you know, I'm a girl."

"That's bullshit." Tom grimaced. "Sorry. Pardon my French."

"No, you're right, it is. Unfortunately, he was paying for my education, so I didn't have any choice in the matter."

Tom didn't speak for a few minutes. I closed my eyes again and tried to pretend I rode next to a gorgeous man I didn't know every day of my life. A sophisticated woman would know how to keep up her side of a scintillating conversation, but as much as I liked to imagine I was worldly, in reality I was just a tongue-tied small-town girl.

I felt the car slow and turn. I opened my eyes and sat up, looking through the windshield at the beach in front of us as Tom parked in the empty lot.

"This looked like a good place to stop. I didn't want to go too far." He shut down the car and leaned back. "I'm not kidnapping you, in case you were worried."

"No, I didn't think so." *And I'm not sure I would mind*, I thought.

"I don't want your family to wonder where you are. Doesn't someone expect you home?"

I knew what I should say. I should tell him that I'd be missed if I didn't get back soon, because if he did turn out to be a rapist or a murderer, at least he might think twice about making me his victim. Although, here we sat, alone in my car, and nothing would stop him from dragging me into the reeds along the dunes and doing whatever he wanted. So I decided to live recklessly.

"I'm down here by myself, on vacation." I met his eyes. "No one is waiting for me."

Tom frowned. "Not very smart to say that. Especially to someone you just met. What if I were a murderer?"

"I was just thinking that, but then I decided it was too late anyway. In for a dime, in for a dollar." I grinned.

He shook his head, but I saw the beginnings of a smile on his face. "Do you make it a habit of offering your car to strangers? Going off with men you don't know?"

The implied lacking in my virtue stung. "Not that it's any of your damn business, but no, I don't. I was being nice. You looked. . ." I searched for the right phrase. "Alone."

Tom glanced away, over the water. "It was a mistake to come down here. One of those spur-of-the-moment things."

"What do you mean? You're not here with friends?" I'd seen groups of soldiers and even some Marines walking around town. I'd assumed Tom was with one of them.

"No. I'm stationed at Fort Dix, and we're being deployed. . .uh, soon. Vietnam." He rubbed the heel of his hand over the steering wheel. "We got a few days' leave beforehand. I thought it might be fun to come down the shore, so I got on the first bus that was heading this way. It happened to be coming here. But when I went to find a hotel, everything was filled up for tonight. I couldn't even get a place to change out of my uniform so I could sit on the beach."

"That's terrible." I shifted in the seat, bending my leg and turning my back to lean against the door so that I faced Tom. "What are you going to do?"

He took off his envelope cap and ran a hand over his close-cropped hair. "I guess I'll get back on the bus and see if I can find a motel some place near post. I don't want to sleep in the barracks when I don't have to."

I looked at his profile, the vivid blue eyes so serious now, firm jaw set and full lips pressed together in a straight line. The smart thing to do at this point would be to drive back to where he'd met me near the beach, say good-bye and go home to the quiet house. It was the safe choice, exactly what a well brought-up girl would do. Of course, that well-brought up girl wouldn't have let a strange man drive her car in the first place, so maybe I was already across that line.

"Do you want to have dinner with me?" I stomped down the protests in the back of my mind, the ones that sounded oddly like my mother's voice.

Tom looked at me, surprise etched on his face. "Dinner?"

"Yeah, it's this meal they serve at the end of the day. It's a new thing, all the cool kids are doing it." Being flippant covered my nerves.

"I'm familiar with the concept. But. . .you don't have to do that. You've probably got better things to do than eat with a lonely soldier."

The lonely part stung me. I didn't know anything about the military, or even what was really going on in Vietnam. There were news reports, and I was vaguely aware that we were fighting the Communist threat, but I didn't know anyone who'd gone over there. We saw soldiers now and then in Philadelphia, but they were always in groups, walking down the street or sitting together in a restaurant. I hadn't considered that some of them were a long way from home.

"I actually don't have anything better to do." I offered him a smile. "If I go home now, I'll end up having a peanut butter sandwich on a tray in front of the television. So you'd be saving me from malnutrition. Not to mention boredom."

He considered me for a minute, his lips drawing together and his eyes narrowing. "I told you why I'm at the beach by myself. If you don't mind me asking, why are you on vacation alone?"

I looked away and fiddled with the piping at the edge of the leather car seat. "It's a long story."

When he didn't say anything, I glanced over to see him watching me with expectation. I shook my head. "Okay. I'm divorced." When he still didn't react, I decided it was safe to go on. "My cousin's getting married next weekend, and it was going to be awkward for me to be there, so her mom, my aunt Susan, gave me two weeks at her beach house."

Tom frowned. "Your family bribed you to stay away from a wedding?"

"I guess that's one way to look at it. But honestly, I didn't want to go anyway. So it was a win-win situation."

"Okay." He stared out into the ocean again, and his tongue darted out to touch the corner of his lips. I wondered if it were a nervous gesture.

"Look, don't think you have to eat dinner with me. I'll be fine." When had this turned around so that I was the pathetic figure?

"It's not that." He hiked up his arm to rest on the back of my seat, and his wrist was at my eye level. I studied the fine hair on the back of his hand and wondered how just seeing a man's forearm could make me feel a little giddy. Maybe Aunt Susan's neighbor was right after all about my needs. With no small effort, I pulled my attention back to what Tom was saying.

"It's not that at all. I'm just not sure of the bus schedule and how late the last one leaves to get me back to post. If I miss it, I'll be sleeping on a park bench tonight, and the Army would frown on me getting picked up for vagrancy right before we deploy."

I spoke without thinking. "You could sleep at my house."

This time, there was no mistaking Tom's shock. "What?"

"I know it's crazy, and maybe I am, too. Crazy, that is. But my aunt's house is big, and it's got four bedrooms, and I only need one, so why should you—a man leaving to defend our country—have to sleep on a bench or even in a cheap motel? And if you murder me in my sleep, well, then I guess I'll have learned my lesson." I knew babbling wasn't attractive, but I couldn't stop myself.

His eyes didn't move from my face. "I'm not going to murder you in your sleep. But what will people think if they find out you let a stranger stay with you overnight?"

"Who's going to find out?" I lifted my shoulder. "My aunt's neighbors? And why would I care about that?"

"Your reputation?"

I laughed. "When you're divorced, you have no reputation. Trust me, no one cares who sleeps with me. I mean, near me."

Tom dropped his hand to rest on the back of my neck, and just the touch of those fingers on my skin made my heart skip around in my chest. I wanted to lean my head back and caress it against his fingers, but I stopped myself.

"I'm sure that's not true. I appreciate you offering me a bed to sleep in, but I don't want people to talk about you." He withdrew his hand and started up the car again. "Why don't we start with dinner, and then see what happens?"

I pivoted to face forward again. "Okay. We'll have to go to my aunt's house first, though, because I can't go in this." I gestured to my cover-up. "You can sit out front in the car if you want. You know, to save my reputation."

He shot me a look full of reproach. "Just tell me how to get there."

When we pulled into the driveway of the white Cape Cod house, none of the neighbors were outside. It was dinner time, after all, and I was sure all of the regulars were either cooking or already out on the boardwalk.

I opened my door and climbed out, reaching in the back for the beach bag. Tom stayed in the driver's seat for a minute, looking up and down the street as though checking for peeping eyes.

"You know, you sitting out here in the car is going to look odder to Aunt Susan's neighbors than you actually coming inside with me."

He considered that before nodding and following me to the front porch. I fumbled to find my keys in the front pocket of the bag.

"Here, let me." Tom reached in and snagged the ring. He leaned around me and unlocked the door, pushing it open so that I could go ahead of him into the living room.

I hit the light switch and pointed to the sofa. "Have a seat and make yourself at home. Do you want something to drink? I've got some beer in the refrigerator."

He perched on the edge of one the easy chairs that faced the television set. "Uh, sure. That sounds good."

I swung into the kitchen and detached a can from the six-pack that Uncle Larry had so kindly left for me. "Is the can okay or do you want me to pour into a glass?

"The can is good." His voice was much closer behind me, and I jumped. I hadn't heard him step into the kitchen and lean against the counter behind me.

"Here you go." I peeled the tab from the top and handed it to him. "There're pretzels, too." I opened a cupboard and set the box on the table.

"Thanks." He took a long gulp of the beer, and I watched his throat work as he swallowed. My eyes swept down the length of his body, tall and hard under the cotton of the uniform. His arms were muscled and his shoulders broad. I wondered if his chest was as firm as the rest of him. His gaze met mine and held, and the air between us seemed to crackle with electricity.

I shook my head to clear it. "I'm going to go clean up and change." I ran my eyes down his uniform. "Did you want to put on something else?"

He looked down as if only now remembering what he was wearing. "Uh, no. I'll stay in this. Just in case anyone saw me come in—I don't want them thinking. . .you know."

I nodded. "Okay. I'll be back out in a few minutes. The ballgame's probably on TV if you want to check."

I turned and fled down the hall to my bedroom before I was tempted to do something I knew would be a bad idea.

A quick bath took care of the sand that still clung to my feet and legs. I spent a few minutes shaving my legs again, even while I scolded myself for letting my mind wander down the path of what could be. The scolding didn't take though, since as I rubbed my favorite scented lotion over my body, part of me was imagining the soldier two rooms over touching me instead.

I watched myself in the bathroom mirror. I'd inherited long legs from my father's side of the family, and I liked showing them off in the short dresses that were all the rage now. My hips were wide and generous in comparison with the small waist above them. From my mother, I'd gotten what my ex-husband had referred to as a killer rack. I pushed my breasts together, trying to picture other hands on them. Just the thought sent a new sort of thrill up my spine.

I'd brought just one good dress down the shore with me, but it was my favorite, a simple black sheath that hit my legs about four inches above the knee. The neckline was modest, but it fit my chest like a glove, showcasing my boobs to their best advantage. I rolled stockings up my legs and attached them to the garter belt that sat below my waist. I slid my feet into black heels and reached for my hairbrush, running it through my long hair. James had tried to talk me into cutting my blonde hair short, like so many of my friends had done, but in that one area I'd rebelled, refusing to give in. I was glad that I could still twist it into a simple chignon on the back of my head.

I dabbed Chanel Number 5 behind my ears, on each wrist, and then, because my nerves were jumping and I needed to be just a little daring, I touched the dropper between my breasts. I took a deep breath and stepped out into the hallway, one hand to my fluttering stomach.

Tom had turned on the television set and sat with his back to me, holding the can of beer loosely in one hand between his knees. When he heard my heels clicking on the tile behind me, he stood up and turned. The little bit of fussing I had done was immediately worth every second when his eyes widened and his mouth drooped.

"Wow. You. . ." He swallowed hard. "You're gorgeous."

My face warmed, and I smiled. "Thanks. Well, I needed to bring my A game. Not every night I'm escorted to dinner by a dashing soldier."

He grinned. "Dashing. That's a first." He drained the rest of his beer and moved past me to drop the can into the trashcan in the kitchen. "So do you know where you want to eat?"

I shook my head. "I really don't. When I've been down here with my family, we usually cook at home or eat at the seafood shack on the boardwalk." I met his eyes. "We can go there if you want, but Saturday night on the boardwalk is going to be crowded."

"I have an idea. I'm not sure, but. . .when I was growing up and came here with my parents, there was a little Greek place, about three blocks off the beach, I think. It was a family restaurant, but I remember the food was really good."

I spread my hands in front of me, palms up, and smiled. "I'm game if you are."

"Okay." He held out his hand to me. "Shall we?"

This time I didn't pause. "Oh, yes."

We locked the house behind us, and Tom dug into his pocket. "Here're the keys."

I glanced at him, my eyebrows raised. "Don't you want to drive?"

He laughed. "Sure, but it's your car. I wouldn't assume I'm taking the wheel."

I reached up and used both of my hands to close his fingers back around the keys. "I would appreciate it if you would." Still holding his hand between mine, I added, "Most men would assume. Thank you for being different."

Tom looked down at me, his blue eyes unreadable in the dimming evening light. I dropped my hands finally, and he opened the passenger door. "Do you want me to put up the top so you don't get blown?"

"No, thanks. It's such a beautiful night. I can always fix my hair if I need to."

"Most girls would insist on putting it up. Thank you for being different."

Gladness swelled in my chest, and I smiled as he backed the car out and began driving back toward the beach. The setting sun had left a hint of warmth in the air, and the breeze was pleasant.

Tom muttered to himself as he squinted at the buildings we passed. Every few minutes, he slowed down and peered at whatever looked a little familiar. We went around one block three times before he slammed on the brakes. I twisted around in my seat, relieved to see no one was behind us.

"Aha! There it is." He executed a perfect U-turn in the middle of the road and pulled into an empty spot along the curb. I looked up at the weathered green awning. I could barely read the white lettering that proclaimed the name of the restaurant: AMALTHIA.

"I know it doesn't look like much. If you want to go somewhere else, it's fine." Tom opened my door and stood back, leaving the choice to me, even though I could tell he really wanted to go inside.

I smiled. "Nope, this looks good. I can't remember the last time I had Greek food." Quite possibly never, I thought. James only ate what he called 'real' American food, most of which was hamburgers, meatloaf or fried chicken. And my parents were not the least bit adventurous when it came to eating.

The inside of the restaurant was a little better than the outside. The lighting was dim, but the tables seemed to be clean. They were covered in checked cloths, with red candle holders in the center, and most of them were filled, which I took as a good sign. A pretty dark-haired woman greeted us.

"Welcome. Table for two?"

Tom slid his eyes to me, and I nodded. His hand came up to press the small of my back as we followed the hostess, and for the first time in years, I felt the pleasure of being cared for by a man.

The menu was printed on a thick plastic booklet. None of the words were familiar to me in the least. I pretended to study the choices, and then I closed the menu and leaned forward.

"Tom, I have a confession to make."

A furrow appeared between his eyebrows. "All right. What is it?"

I took a deep breath. "I've never had Greek food. I have no idea what any of this is."

His shoulders relaxed, and he grinned at me. "Is that all? Don't worry. I'll order for you." He dropped his voice down to nearly a whisper. "Do you trust me?"

I reached across the table to lay my hand on top of his. "I let you drive my car two minutes after we met. I invited you to dinner and to sleep at my house. I think that qualifies as trust, don't you?"

Tom's eyes bore deep into mine. "I'd say so. But do you trust me when it comes to choosing your food?"

I didn't look away. "Absolutely."

And he didn't let me down. He pointed to items on the menu, and the young woman who served us smiled and nodded in approval.

"And ouza for both us." Tom winked at the waitress as he handed her the menus. I caught the look on her face as she walked toward the kitchen.

"What's ouza?"

He sat back in his chair. "I thought you trusted me."

"I do, but I like to know what I'm eating. No snails or bugs, right?"

He chuckled. "No, and it's not something to eat. It's a Greek drink."

I tilted my head, letting my lips curl. "Why, sir, are you planning on getting me intoxicated tonight?"

The way Tom's eyes darkened made my chest constrict. His tongue came out again and licked his lips, but he didn't answer me.

The waitress returned with a decorated bottle and two small glasses. She poured the milky liquid as she said, "Stin uyeia sou!"

"What does that mean?" I asked Tom after she left.

He shook his head. "No idea, but probably 'cheers' or something like that." He lifted his glass. "So, here's to. . ." He paused, letting his eyes roam over my face. "Beautiful women."

I picked up my own drink. "And to kind gentlemen." I sampled the liquid with caution, but when I realized that it tasted like licorice, I tossed back the entire glass.

"Hey there, slow down." Tom set down his own empty shot. "It won't look good if I have to carry you out of here."

I giggled, feeling the burn of the liquor down my throat and to the tips of my fingers. "What's the matter, afraid you couldn't handle it?"

He captured my hand, closing his fingers around mine. "No, I could handle it."

I turned my wrist so that our palms touched. "I've never been carried anywhere before. In a night of new experiences, that may be the best one yet."

Tom tightened his grip on my hand. "New experiences are. . ." He dropped his voice. "Exciting."

I wasn't sure how to answer, and I was saved from coming up with anything when the server brought us a plate filled with some kind of leaf-wrapped packets. Tom told me what they were and how to eat them, and within moments I was moaning.

"These are so good. What do you call them again?"

"Dolmathakia. I'm glad you like them." He finished chewing and laid his fork across the small white plate. "Caroline, can I ask you something?"

"Sure." I tipped the bottle of ouza over my glass again.

"Why are you divorced?"

I set the bottle down on the table with a thunk. Any other time, this question would have made me bristle, but tonight, with the protective glow of the liquor, I only rolled my eyes.

"Let's see. Lots of reasons. First, I married the wrong man. I thought I loved him, and I thought he loved me, but I was mistaken on both counts. And second, because I wasn't a very good wife. And finally, the prime reason I'm divorced—" I snickered and put my finger in front of my lips, shushing Tom as though it were he talking too loudly. "The number one reason is that my husband got another girl pregnant, and I wasn't okay with that."

"My God. I'm sorry." Tom took my hand again, and this time, I threaded our fingers together.

"Don't be. I'm not. I mean, the timing was kind of bad, but a year later, I can see that it was really for the best."

"Why was the timing bad?" He slipped his thumb between our hands to rub tantalizing circles on my palm. "I wouldn't think there'd be a good time for that kind of announcement."

"It was our wedding anniversary, and I was waiting at home. I'd made a beautiful dinner. Put on. . ." I hunched over and whispered the next word. "Lingerie. You know, because I was hoping for romance."

Tom nodded. "Uh huh."

"And instead, he came home and told me that he'd knocked up his secretary. I mean, how cliché can you get? His secretary. All this time I thought there was something wrong with me because he never wanted me in the. . ." I lifted a finger of my free hand and twirled it in the air. "You know. The bedroom. I thought I just wasn't exciting enough. And I guess I wasn't because he had to sleep with her. If I'd been a better wife, and maybe better in the bedroom, he wouldn't have had to do that."

"Caroline, that's bullshit."

"Yeah? Well, it's what my mother said. And his mother, and my aunts, and my friends. A real woman can keep a husband. Divorce is failure."

Tom laid our joined hands on the table and gripped me harder. "Like I said, bullshit. My aunt's divorced. She said it was the best thing that ever happened to her. It gave her a new life. It doesn't mean she failed. It just means she made a decision to be happy." One side of his mouth turned up into a smile. "At least that's what she says."

I leaned my cheek against my hand, elbow resting on the table. "I don't know why I'm even talking about this with you. We don't know each other at all. And I never talk about my marriage."

"Maybe that's why. Maybe a complete stranger can see you more clearly than all of your family and friends."

I opened my mouth, but whatever I was going to say was forgotten when the next course appeared. I was quiet until the waitress walked away again.

"Why did you join the Army?" I used my fork to cut off a chunk of pastry stuffed with spinach and cheese. Tom had called it spano-something, and it was heavenly.

He slid a piece of lamb off the skewer on his plate. "It's a long story. And kind of painful."

"Hey, I just told you that my husband got his secretary pregnant. There are no secrets here. You owe me one."

Tom chewed, regarding me steadily. I held his eyes, not moving until he'd swallowed and finished off his ouza.

"Okay." He placed the fork onto the side of his plate. "I was in love. Or I thought I was. Molly was the most perfect, exciting, beautiful girl I'd ever met. She was smart and funny and we had so much in common. She was also my best friend's girlfriend."

"Ooooh." I winced. "Sticky, huh?"

"Yeah, you could say. We all met in college. And I convinced myself that eventually, Molly would end things with Phil. She didn't, and last year, he proposed to her. She said yes, of course, and then one night, when Phil was away for work and I'd taken Molly out to eat, I got drunk and I told her how I felt. That she couldn't marry him, because I loved her."

"Oh my God." I covered my mouth. "What did she say?"

"She said I was an idiot, and she loved Phil. Always had. She didn't see me as anything more than a friend. The next day, she called me to say that we should never mention this to Phil, ever, and that I needed to stick around for their wedding and then go away. I enlisted that day."

"Did you go to the wedding?" I pushed back my plate. I'd discovered I liked Greek food, but God, it was filling.

He nodded. "I got leave. I went, and I was a wonderful best man. I made the toasts, kissed the bride on the cheek, and left. As far as I know, Phil never suspected a thing."

"I'm sorry." I sat back in my chair, studying him. The intriguing blue eyes were set in angular face, with a straight nose and high cheekbones. In the candlelight, I could just make out the vaguest shadow of stubble on his cheeks. His bottom lip was full, and for one moment of insanity, all I wanted to do was lean over the table and kiss him.

"Will you stay with me tonight?" The words tumbled out of my mouth, but I didn't regret them. Sitting here, in this circle of flickering light, I felt as though we were in a world removed from reality, set apart from consequences and expectations.

Those blue eyes didn't flinch from my face. "Are you sure that's a good idea?"

"I'm not sure of anything, but I think that's okay. This is just. . ." I cast my eyes up to the ceiling, thinking. "A fluke. Something that happened now and never will again. Tomorrow you'll go back to Fort Dix, and I'll finish my vacation here. We'll never see each other again."

I noticed that Tom wasn't protesting what might or might not happen between the two of us. "But what if there's fallout? If one of your neighbors sees me and talks about it? I don't want to make more trouble for you with your family."

"They don't care. And I'd only be living up to what they all think, apparently." I ran the tip of my tongue over my top lip. "Don't you know what they say about divorcees? We have needs. And the men are lining up to help us with that little problem."

His eyes turned to flint. "Who the hell said that to you?"

"Who didn't? Let's start with my ex-husband's friends, then move on to my own friends' husbands. My aunt's neighbor." I leaned forward again, lowering my voice. "When you're divorced, it means you're not an innocent anymore, so you must be a whore. Right?"

"Fuck that." Tom spoke quietly, too, but with an intensity that flooded my chest with an unfamiliar sensation. I thought it might be desire.

"I'm not." It was somehow important that he understood. "After James left, I moved back home with my parents. I didn't have any place else to go. But I haven't been with anyone."

"It shouldn't matter. Your bastard of a husband left you, so why should you have to pay the price?" He paused and picked up my hand yet again, this time with a gentleness that made me want to weep. "What's he doing now, by the way? The husband? Does his family treat him like a pariah, too?"

I snorted. "Hardly. He married the secretary as soon as our divorce was final. Their little boy was born five months ago. They live in the house he bought me, and she drives my car."

"That's how you got the Mustang, isn't it?"

"That was my one reward, yes. I didn't want anything from him, but my father, bless him, insisted on alimony and the car. I decided if I were going to get one, I might as well have something really bitchin'."

The waitress stepped up to hand Tom the check. I dug into my purse, but he stilled me with a look.

"If I'm going to sleep at your house tonight, the least I can do is buy you dinner."

I felt my cheeks grow red, and I nodded.

He tucked a few bills into the black leather folder and handed it to our passing server with a smile, telling her to keep the change. When he rose, I stood up, too, taking his hand as though it were the most natural thing in the world.

"Thank you for dinner." I turned to step in front of Tom when the restaurant door closed behind us. Standing on my toes, I brushed my lips across his cheek, letting my breasts tease against his chest. He caught my arms in his two hands, keeping my face close to his as he stared down at me. I thought he was going to kiss me, but instead he only tilted his head to my ear.

"You're welcome."

He released me and held my door again. The night had cooled considerably, and I shivered a little as the sea air blew across my shoulders. Tom, sliding behind the steering wheel, glanced at me.

"I have a jacket in my duffel if you want it."

"Thanks. I think I'm all right." Another gust hit me, and my teeth might have chattered just a little.

"Here." He turned in his seat, and I heard the click of metal as he unlatched the duffel bag. I watched the play of muscles in his back under the uniform shirt, and suddenly I wasn't so chilly anymore.

He shook out a cotton jacket. "Lean up."

I moved forward, away from the seat, and he draped it around me, pulling the material to meet in the front. His knuckles brushed my nipples, and I drew in a sharp breath.

"Sorry." He brought his hands up beneath my chin, flipping the collar of the jacket up. He touched my jaw with his two thumbs, and before I could move, his lips covered mine.

It had been so long since I'd been kissed. Even in the last few months of my marriage, I couldn't remember James doing more than touching his lips to my cheek when he left for work.

But what Tom did to me was like nothing I'd ever experienced. His lips sealed against mine, pressing just enough that I could feel the bristle of his scruff against the skin above my mouth. He moved a fraction of an inch, so that I could feel the gentle suction before his tongue traced the outline of my lips.

I lifted my hand to the side of his face, feeling the movement of his jaw. His skin was warm, and when I ran my fingers up into his hair, the short hairs tickled.

Tom groaned against my mouth at my touch and used his thumbs to press down on my chin, coaxing my mouth open. Once my lips parted, his tongue ventured within, parrying with mine in a dance that made me want more.

He broke away from me just long enough to kiss across my cheek to my ear. "Caroline."

"Yes?" I knew I sounded breathless, but I couldn't help it. My heart was pounding a staccato against my rib cage, and breathing had lost its priority.

"If I don't take us to your house now, I'm going to drag you into the back seat and have the kind of make-out session that used to get me in trouble when I was a teenager. Right here, in front of the restaurant. I want you so bad I can't think of not touching you."

"Oh." His words laid me out, wide open and bare, willing to let him do anything he wanted, anywhere.

"So you need to tell me to drive. Now."

"Tom?"

"Yeah?"

"When we get back to my house, will you kiss me again?"

His laugh rumbled against my ear, and then he sucked my earlobe into his mouth, catching it between his teeth. I felt his tongue press against the sensitive flesh before he released it.

"Baby, just try to stop me."

"Tom. Drive. Now."

He fell back into the driver's seat and turned the key. I snuggled down, clutching his jacket around me and breathing in his scent until I was dizzy as he pulled away from the curb and sped through the dark streets. I was too worked up to talk, but I leaned forward and turned on the radio. Barbara Lewis's voice poured out of the speakers, her sensuous words a vow that made me shake with anticipation.

Baby, I'm yours. . .

Since we knew where we were going this time, it didn't take as long to get back to Aunt Susan's as it had to drive to the restaurant. Tom cruised up the driveway into the carport and killed the engine. For a few beats of my heart, we sat in the sudden quiet, shadows hiding our faces.

"Caroline, are you sure?"

I knew what he meant. He wasn't asking if I were certain about him coming inside and spending the night in one of the empty bedrooms. He wanted to know if I wanted him in my bed, touching me. Inside my body.

I didn't hesitate. "Yes." I gripped the leather seat and closed my eyes. "I know this can't be anything more than just one night. I know you're leaving tomorrow, and I'll never see you again. But I want tonight. I'm tired of being alone, and if only for right now, I want more. I want it all."

I heard the creak as Tom shifted in his seat, and then I felt his warm breath on my neck. "You are the most beautiful woman I've ever seen, and I don't want to ruin this by mentioning him, but your ex-husband was a fucking idiot if he couldn't see how lovely and. . ." He touched his lips to the pulse at the base of my throat. ". . .desirable you are. You should never have to be alone if you don't want to be. Even if it's just for tonight, I want to be the man who makes you know all of that. The one who makes you feel it."

I brushed my hand over his face. "Let's go inside."

Tom opened his door, this time snagging his bag from the back. I didn't wait for him to come around to my side. Instead, I met him on the porch as I unlocked the house. He kept his hand pressed to my lower back, and I expected that when I took off my dress, I'd see the imprint burned onto my skin.

We stepped into the living room, and Tom turned the lock. My eyes took a few minutes to adjust to the dark, but I heard the clink as he dropped his duffel on the floor. He knelt next to it for a minute, fumbling with the opening, and I thought he might have stuffed something into his pocket. He stood up and stepped close, dropping his hands to just above my ass and holding me close enough that I could feel the hardness between his legs.

"Can I ask you something?" His lips were back at my ear, this time tracing the shell with his tongue.

"Ah. . ." I sighed, my knees threatening to buckle. "Yeah. Anything."

"You said before. . .things with your husband weren't great in the bedroom."

I dropped my forehead to his chest. "Mmmhmmm."

"Hey." He tipped my chin up with one finger. "I just want to know. Did. . .he take care of you? I mean. . .did you come?"

I brought my hand between us, entwining my fingers with his. "Come where?"

"Oh, baby." He tugged me closer, until every soft part of my body was crushed against his hard planes. "He never gave you an orgasm? Made you climax?"

I frowned. "I don't know what you mean. God, I'm stupid, aren't I?"

"No, you were with a stupid man. Here, take my hands. Show me where he touched you. What he did." He gave me his other hand, and I matched our palms together, hesitating, all of a sudden shy.

"He. . .would start. . .here." I drew in our joined hands to my breasts. "He. . .squeezed. Sometimes. . ." I turned my fingers in so that our joined knuckles skimmed over my nipples. "Here. And that felt good. If he wasn't too rough."

Tom made a sound low in his chest, almost a growl. "Did he hurt you?"

"No." I shook my head. "Not like that. Not on purpose. But there were times when he just didn't know how to be soft, I guess. Maybe he thought it was what I wanted."

"Okay. And then what?"

"Ah. . ." I cast my mind back. I had pushed those memories so far away that bringing them near again felt like picking at a nearly-healed scab. "Then most of the time, he just took off my underwear." I swallowed hard. "And he finished. You know." I bit my lip, thinking. "A few times, in the beginning, he took my hand and made me touch him. I didn't know how, but I wanted to do the right thing. And then right after our honeymoon, he got impatient one night and said I didn't know anything."

"Son of a bitch." Tom broke one hand free and cupped my cheek. My eyes were getting used to the darkness, and I could see the outlines of his face and the shine of his eyes as he stared. "Did he expect you to be a virgin when he married you?"

I nodded, glad he couldn't see the blush I was certain had stained my face. "Of course."

"Didn't you ever talk about it? What would happen after you got married? Or didn't your mother tell you anything, or your friends?"

"James never talked about anything that happened in the bedroom. And my mother—she would never bring that up. I got married before most of my friends, but even then, we didn't ever discuss it. And it was just, you know." I shrugged. "What you had to do. But it seemed to me like there should be more."

"Baby, there's a lot more." Tom fitted his hands around the curve of my ass and lifted me until our faces were level. "So much more." He kissed me, open-mouthed and hungry, and I couldn't do anything but respond. "Let me show you."

"Yes." I threaded my fingers together in the back of his head. "Please."

He walked down the hallway, his mouth still devouring me. He shifted one hand to my thigh and nudged it until I wrapped both legs around his waist. The bottom of my dress hiked up, and there was only the thin layer of my panties between me and the ridge of flesh I felt beneath his zipper.

Tom kicked open the door to my bedroom and fell onto the bed with me. He stood and began unbuttoning the shirt of his uniform. I rose up to lean on my elbows, watching him.

"First, I'm going to make you come." His eyes never left mine as he draped the shirt over the back of the chair that was pushed up against the wall. "And then I'm going to teach you what it should be like between a man and woman, so you'll never expect anything less."

I drank in the sight of his chest, all muscles and tanned skin, and the tightness of his stomach. A thin line of light brown hair ran down and disappeared into his pants, and my fingers itched to follow its path. As though he knew what I was thinking, his fingers unhooked the trousers, and he stepped out of them, laying them on top of the shirt. He stood before me in only his boxers, his erection straining the placket.

"I feel very overdressed." I began to sit up, but Tom stopped me with a hand to my shoulder.

"No, let me." He reached behind me and found the zipper tab, pulling it down my back with maddening slowness. I shivered, and my eyes drifted closed. He bought his fingers up to my shoulders and eased the top of the dress until it was at my elbows, pinning my arms to my sides.

"Lay down." He let go of me, and I fell back onto the bed, my heart pounding as I wondered what would come next. Tom nudged my knees apart so that he stood between them, his fingertips tickling over my thighs. He found the tops of my stockings, disconnected them from my garter belt and eased both of them down my legs.

I tried not to let myself shake when he slid back onto his heels, crouching to take off my shoes and letting my stockings follow. With one finger, he outlined the arch of my foot, and then I felt his tongue follow in its wake. His mouth never left my skin as he moved his lips over my ankle and up my calf, pausing at my knee to suck on the tender skin in the back. The intimate touch sent a shock of wild current up to the juncture of my legs, and I felt a surge of wetness there.

I was mortified, wondering how I could stop him from continuing up and discovering my shame. His tongue drew small intoxicating circles along my inner thigh, and he reached his hand to touch between my legs, gentle and seeking. He ran one finger up and down over the silk that covered me, damp with my own essence, and I opened my mouth to try to apologize. But before I could speak, Tom groaned.

"Caroline—oh, baby. You're so wet for me. God, that turns me on." He slipped two fingers under my panties, touching me, and I cried out, bucking my hips upward, unable to control myself.

"God—Tom—oh, God—" Something was beating within in me, some unfamiliar pressure building low in my abdomen and centered there where Tom touched me. I didn't know if I was going to die or explode, but I couldn't breathe, couldn't stop from arching into his hand as one finger skimmed deeper into the top of my folds. And then he pressed his thumb there, and at the same time, slipped two fingers inside me.

Everything in the world burst into flame, colors in vivid stars appearing before my eyes as my awareness shrunk down to that one part of my body and Tom's fingers. I heard a cry as his name ripped from my own throat, and I gripped madly at the bed cover beneath me.

I was only vaguely aware of Tom sliding my underwear down my legs a few moments later. The bed dipped, but I didn't have the strength to turn my head toward him. He kissed my neck, murmuring words I couldn't quite make out until he came to my mouth again. He touched my lips, stroked the inside of my mouth with his tongue, and then moved to my ear, where he suckled on the lobe again, making me sigh.

"Was that good?" At his whisper, my mouth tilted up into a smile I couldn't hide.

"Oh. My. God. That was. . ." I managed to open my eyes and met his. "I didn't know. All that time. . .that I could feel like this."

"That was an orgasm, baby. That was me, making you come. It happened fast just now, because you haven't been touched in so long. But I'm going to do it again, and again, and then again before the night is over."

"I'm not sure I can." It felt like every nerve of my body was hyper-sensitive, and the idea of him touching me more might put me into sensory overload.

"Oh, you can. And you will." He kissed me again, leaning his body over mine, and I felt his hardness against my thigh.

"Is what happened to me just now the same thing that men feel when they. . .?" I wasn't sure how to describe it. I remembered with James, it had almost seemed as though he were in pain as his body tensed and jerked into mine, but afterward, he'd always seemed grateful.

Tom laughed, his breath soft on my neck. "Yeah, pretty much." He slipped his fingers under my head and his eyes squinted as he felt for my hairpins. He pulled three out and then lifted my head to free my hair and spread it beneath me. "Your hair's like silk, you know that? Just beautiful."

I laid my hand on his cheek and rubbed my thumb over his full bottom lip. "If that's what it feels like, I understand now why guys all are so interested."

"That's only the beginning." He pushed up on his hands, and sitting next to my hip, took my dress the rest of the way off my arms and then down my body. He looked down at me, and I swore the blue of his eyes deepened as he took in the lace garter belt still around my hips and the swell of skin over the cups of my bra. "God, Caroline. You're. . .I don't have the words. Look at you. You're perfect." He bent over me and touched his lips to the top of one breast.

"Will you. . ." I closed my eyes. "Are you going to touch me there?"

"Where?" The vibration of his voice rumbled over my chest.

"There." I gestured, waving my hand in a circle above my body.

"Caroline." Tom lay down alongside me, leaning on his elbow. "If you want me to do something, you have to ask." He walked his fingers down my sternum. "Sex. . .making love. . .it's a grown-up thing. I'm not going to bring him up again, because tonight is between you and me only, but I am going to say your ex-husband didn't act like an adult with you. He's a selfish, stupid asshole, because a real man takes care of his woman. He makes sure she's safe and satisfied. And a real woman—" He raised one eyebrow and swept his gaze down my body again. "Like you. She knows how to ask for what she needs. She can say the words."

I was certain my face had gone crimson. "So you want me to ask you to—" I swallowed. "Touch my breast?"

I was afraid he would laugh, but he only moved his hand a little closer. "That works. If you're okay with me just doing this." He laid one finger on top of my bra, nowhere near where I wanted it. "Is that what you want?"

Shaking my head, I took a deep breath. "Will you touch my nipples?"

A smile spread over his lips. "Oh, yeah, I will." He circled the rigid tips over the top of the thick bra material, and I wanted to scream.

"No. *Under* the bra. Touch my skin."

"That's it." He pushed back the cup on one side and teased my nipple, sending tremors down my body. When he moved to the other side, he dropped closer to me, his mouth hovering near the pink nub his fingers had just abandoned.

"Do you want me to kiss you here, Caroline? Suck on your nipple? You could even ask me to suck your tits, if you like that word better."

"I've never used that word in my life." I pressed against the back of his head. "But yes."

"Tell me. Words, remember. It's only you and me here. There's no reason to be embarrassed. Hearing you saying it only makes me want you more."

This time I kept my eyes open and watched Tom as I spoke. "Suck on my nipples, please. Kiss my—tits."

He didn't hesitate to cover one nipple with his mouth, sucking it between his teeth and letting his tongue circle the tip until I moaned. He reached under my back and unhooked my bra, tossing it out of the way.

"Caroline, you have got the most incredible tits I've ever seen." He palmed them, bringing the white globes together as his mouth laved one nipple and his fingers pinched the other. "Tell me how it makes you feel when I do this."

"It makes me. . ." I couldn't think of how to describe the feeling. "Like there's a direct line from my—my tits to, umm, lower. Between my legs," I finished, proud that I hadn't chickened out on naming it.

"Your pussy?" Tom moved his mouth to my other breast. "Does it make your pussy wet when I suck your tits?"

Part of me wanted to laugh. All that time, married two years and I'd never so much as asked James to touch me in any particular way. Fleetingly I wondered what he would've said if I'd told him to touch my pussy. Most of me didn't care anymore.

"Pussy." I repeated the word. "That's what you call it? Okay. Yes, it makes my pussy extremely wet when you suck my tits. That's a good thing, right?"

"It really is." Tom slid down me, kissing a path from the bottom of my boobs down my stomach. "When a woman is wet there, it means she's turned on. She's ready." He continued down, stopping at my navel to swirl his tongue there, while his hand stayed at my nipple, alternately caressing and rubbing between his finger and thumb. When he slid down lower, I startled, sitting up until I could see him.

"What are you doing?" I touched the top of his head, trying to get a grip on any hair and make him stop. It was too short for me to pull, but he looked up at me anyway, a wicked smile on his face.

"Don't you trust me?' He laid his head against my hip and trailed one finger until it dipped into my core. I gasped and dropped my head back to dangle between my shoulders.

"Yes." I could barely speak while his finger moved over my slick flesh. "But—what are you going to do?"

"I told you I was going to make you come again. See, that's the cool thing about women. When a man climaxes, it takes him a little while to recover, to be able to get hard again. But a woman can have lots of orgasms and still want more. So I'm going to make you come again, like this, and then when I'm inside of you, I'm going to do it again." He brushed a kiss high on my inner thigh. "You're going to make up for lost time tonight, sweetheart."

"Oh, God." The fire was building again as Tom explored me with just one finger.

"Caroline, open your eyes. Look at me."

I lifted my head and met his gaze. My chest rose and fell as I panted.

"I'm going to use my mouth on your pussy. Don't freak out on me. Just watch." He dropped his lips between my legs, and I thought my heart would stop beating. Seeing him kiss me there, feeling his mouth in that most unexpected place, was pushing me dangerously close to the edge again.

He paused for a minute, looking up at me again. "I want you to know what I'm doing, so you can ask for it. Don't ever be afraid or ashamed to ask for what you want, Caroline." He parted me a little more with his fingers and used just one to circle a spot at the top of my folds.

"Right here is your clit. It should feel incredible when I touch you here." He pressed the small nub lightly, and I moaned as my eyes drifted close again.

"No, baby, open your eyes. I need you to see this." He brought his mouth down again, and this time his lips surrounded my clit and sucked. When his tongue darted out to lick against it too, I couldn't help myself. I cried out his name and dropped my shoulders back onto the mattress, my eyes screwed shut as waves of unadulterated pleasure swept over me. My hips jerked against his mouth, but Tom didn't stop. He held my ass, bringing me closer to his mouth, as though he couldn't get enough, and I felt his groan as his tongue delved inside me, moving in time with the spasms that consumed my entire body.

He gentled his lips, kissing and stroking as my heartbeat slowed and the climax subsided to aftershocks. I couldn't move a muscle as he kissed his way back up to my face. When I opened my eyes again, he was leaning over me, watching.

"Hi." He covered my lips with his, and I tasted something new and different on his mouth—my own juices. It wasn't bad, just foreign.

"Hi, yourself." I rallied enough strength to hold his face in both of my hands. "Tom, that was incredible. I can't believe I've lived so much of my life not knowing about how amazing this could be."

"And we've only just begun." He held himself over me, and I felt his erection against my still-sensitive pussy. It was hard and seemed impossibly large.

I slid my hands down his neck, over his shoulders, letting my fingers stroke his chest and down to his abdomen. He was all muscle and sinew, and his strength made me want all over again, even when I'd thought every ounce of my energy had been sapped.

"Do I touch you now?" I reached the top of his boxers, but I wasn't sure what to do next. After all the pleasure I'd experienced, I was eager to make him feel just as good. I had no idea how to go about making it happen.

"Baby, there is no right or wrong way here, unless it's something that hurts you or feels wrong." Tom dropped down next to me. "Tell you what. I'll lay here, still as I can, and you do whatever comes to mind. Don't be afraid, okay?"

"Don't you have to use your words, too? To tell me what feels good?" I sat up, cross-legged, looking down at his body as it lay before me.

"Sweetheart, all you have to do right now is breathe on me, and it's going to feel incredible. But you're right, you should know the right terms. So you do what you want, and I'll tell you what you're doing."

"Okay." I smiled a little and bent myself nearly in two to start at his lips. I kissed him with my mouth closed at first, and then I let my tongue venture out to run over the line of his lip. When he parted for me, I leaned in further and thrust my tongue deeper, circling his and then stroking, mimicking what he had done earlier. He tangled his hands in my hair, keeping me close.

"Baby, when you kiss me, the world pretty much ends. I could lay here for days, just doing this."

I smiled and trailed down his neck. "But then I'd never learn anything, would I?" I pressed my palm to his chest, covering the flat disc of his nipple. Curiosity took over, and I pinched the nub between my finger and thumb as he had done to mine. When he hissed in a breath, I grinned.

"That feels good to you, too?"

"Yeah. Yeah, it does."

Deciding to be daring, I scooted down a little further on the bed and angled myself over Tom, replacing my fingers with my lips. He made a low sound of approval deep in his chest.

"What do I call this?" I caught one nipple between my teeth and worried it there, then licked all around. "I'm thinking it's not boobs or tits."

His chest shook as he chuckled. "Not so much. Not in this context. Just nipples. And chest." He tickled the back of my neck with his thumb. "And baby, I love it when you suck my nipples and touch my chest. It makes me even harder."

I let my eyes wander down to where his boxers strained. I was nervous about touching him there, because I knew I hadn't pleased James when I'd tried. The idea of disappointing Tom made me want to cry.

As if he'd read my mind, he touched my cheek until I looked up at him again. "Caroline, don't be afraid. There is nothing you can do that isn't going to give me pleasure. Forget what the idiot might have said. You are fucking sexy. Don't doubt that, ever."

I couldn't speak, but I nodded, letting my hands venture down the tantalizing muscles of his stomach to the waistband of his boxers. Taking a deep breath, I slipped one hand inside.

My first thought was that he was warm. My fingertips met coarse hair, and then I touched him, lightly stroking the shaft. I circled my fingers around to hold him, surprised at the thickness within my hand. Experimenting, I moved my fist up and down, holding just tight enough to feel the steel beneath the soft of his skin.

"Caroline, feeling your hand on my cock is the best fucking thing in the world. God, don't stop."

My face flushed with pleasure at his groaned words. Bold now, I stopped just long enough to tug down his boxers, sliding them over his feet and tossing them to the pile of clothes on the floor.

Now that I could see him, I brought both hands onto his cock, using one to hold him firmly at the base and the other to circle the springy head. A clear drop of liquid poised at the top, and I ventured to touch it, rubbing it between my fingers and then down the shaft.

My knuckles grazed over the sack below his erection, and I flickered my eyes to his face, testing to see how he reacted. He arched his head back, much as I had done when his mouth had been between my legs.

"Do you like that?"

"Uh, yes. It feels really good when you touch my balls."

Balls. Hmm. I climbed to sit between his legs and gently held his balls with one hand, moving my fingers idly. With the other hand, I held his cock again and stroked, noticing that his hips began to piston when I picked up speed. It made me feel powerful and alive, knowing I was making him feel good, lighting him with the same pleasure that had exploded inside my body a few minutes before.

Thinking of what Tom had done to me gave me an idea. He had told me that I could try anything, and so I didn't even hesitate to bring my mouth to his cock, kissing up the length and letting my tongue draw designs on the musky skin.

"Caroline!" Tom growled, gripping my hair. "You don't have to do that."

I paused, but I didn't sit up. "Don't you like it? Is this wrong?"

He barked out a laugh that sounded like a cross between humor and pain. "Like isn't strong enough a word. Your mouth on my cock is the sweetest thing in the world. But I don't want you to do anything that makes you uncomfortable."

"I'm not. What do you call this?"

"Ah, well, heaven would be my guess right now. But uh, if you take me in your mouth, moving up and down that way, it's called a blow job."

"Oh. Why? Am I supposed to. . .blow on you?"

He shook his head. "No, I don't know why. It's just what it's called. But you don't have to do that. Just what you're doing now is wonderful."

I thought about it, about the intensity of feeling when he'd had his mouth on me, and then sank over him, taking just the tip between my lips. Tom groaned again, so I took more of him, opening my mouth and adjusting until his cock hit the back of my throat. I brought my lips back up, sucking a little along the way. It made me feel powerful and almost Amazonian, seeing how much gratification I was bringing him. Each time I drew up my mouth, I felt a corresponding tug at my own core, making me want with a ferocity I'd never known.

"Caroline." He grunted my name. "God, baby, that is so good. But if you keep it up, I'm going to come. And I want to be inside you when I do that."

I dropped one more kiss to the head and then crawled up his body. "That's really good timing, because I want you in me. Now." I kissed him, open-mouthed and wanton in my desire.

"Hold on." Tom jumped off the bed and crouched on the floor by the chair where his clothes hung, reaching into the pocket. I rolled onto my back and watched him tear open a little foil packet.

"What is that?" I sat up, leaning on my hands.

He glanced up at me, astonishment in his eyes. "It's a condom. Don't tell me you've never seen one."

I shook my head. "I know what it is, but no, I haven't seen it. I mean, not outside the wrapper. A couple of boys in high school used to carry them in their wallets." Before he could ask, I added, "And no, James didn't use them. I'm on the pill."

"I'm glad you are." He rolled the rubber over his jutting cock. "But I don't want to take any chances. Not when I'm leaving to go overseas in a matter of days."

He sat down next to me again with one arm on either side of my body. I lifted my mouth to meet his in another searing kiss, moving my head to give him better access to plunder against my tongue. His hand lifted to cup my breast, and I smiled against his lips as his thumb rubbed over my nipple.

"Tom, I want you to suck my tits and touch my pussy. And then I want you to. . .be inside me. Please."

He laughed, an intimate sound that sent a thrill up my spine. "Right away, baby. You're a fast learner." He turned and shifted so that his knees were between my thighs, and then he lifted my nipple to his mouth. I lay back, mouth open and gasping as he laved the rosy peak, then bit gently. He held his weight off me with one hand, and the other he stroked down my wet center.

"I'm going to get you right to the edge, but don't come. Not yet. Not 'til I'm inside you."

I arched my back, seeking to get even closer to his talented fingers. "How can I stop?"

"Tell me when you're close. When you feel like all it would take is one more touch. . .one more suck. . ." He moved his mouth to the other breast and made circles around my throbbing clit. I laid back and focused on just feeling each and every touch, committing each to my memory.

When he slid two fingers inside me and rubbed my clit harder, I threw back my head. "Now. Oh, now. Right on the edge. Please. . ." I fumbled to reach for him, to pull his hips against mine. "Please, I need you to be inside me."

Tom didn't wait. He centered himself over my entrance, and I felt the head of his cock—that had been in my mouth moments before—probing my pussy. He covered my mouth at the same time, his tongue giving me a preview as it plunged between my lips with no mercy.

"Open your eyes again, Caroline. I want to watch you when you fall apart. And I want you to see me, and only me, when I come inside you."

I fastened onto his face, and as soon as I did, he slid into me on one long, hard thrust. It was the most mind-shattering sensation of my life, so far removed from anything I'd ever experienced before that I wanted to laugh at the comparison and at the same time cry for what I'd been missing. Tom's eyes widened, and he dropped his forehead to rest on mine.

"So, so good, baby. You're fucking tight and you feel perfect. I want to stay like this forever. But I've got to—" He moved, pulling out just a little and then plunging back in. I gripped his backside and wriggled, wanting to feel more, to make him move faster and harder.

Tom rocked into me. "Tell me what you want, Caroline. Use words. Tell me how to make you feel good."

I rotated my hips, undulating to find the best spot. "Make it harder—and oh, God, can you move faster in me—"

"Say it, baby. Tell me to fuck you hard. Tell me you want it."

All pretenses of modesty were shattered. I dug my nails into his back and held his ass with my heels. "God, Tom, fuck me. Fuck me hard and fast. I want you harder, harder."

With a sound I could only describe as a roar, he let go, pounding into me until I screamed, arching and bucking as the universe erupted. My inner muscles clenched in reaction, and Tom followed me, shouting my name, shuddering violently as he climaxed.

He collapsed next to me on the bed, breathing hard. I closed my eyes against the sudden tears gathering there. I had no idea why I would be crying after what I had just experienced. I should have been exulting, flying high.

"Hey." Tom rolled over and gathered me close. "Are you all right?"

"All right? My God, Tom, what we just did—all right doesn't even begin to describe it." I shifted my head on his chest so that I could see his face. "I had no clue. No one ever told me it could be like this. What I had for two years—that was laughable. Like eating bread and water for years and then discovering all the other food that exists in the world."

He laughed. "That's a good way to describe it." He touched my nose with the tip of his finger and then ran it down to my bottom lip. "Baby, you were. . ." He searched my eyes, as a crease formed between his brows. "I don't think there are words for how sexy you are. You remind me of a volcano. You look like a quiet mountain, majestic and still, but then you erupt, and damn." He shook his head. "You blew me away."

I smiled, hiding my face against his arm. "I had a fabulous teacher." Without thinking about it, I spread my hand over his chest, brushing my fingers over the nipple nearest to me. I felt the beat of his heart under my hand pick up speed. "Tom, can I ask you a few things?"

"Of course you can. You can ask me anything. I don't think I could keep anything back from you at this point." He grinned down at his cock, now lying quietly against his stomach. "But give me a minute to clean up, okay?"

My eyes followed him as he stood up, stretching, and removed the condom. He went down the hallway to the bathroom, and I heard the water turn on and off before he sauntered back into the bedroom.

He really was gorgeous. I had never even thought that word in reference to a man before, but there was no denying it in his case. Even walking naked, he moved with a grace and confidence that made me want to drag him back onto the bed and start all over again.

Happily, I didn't have to drag him back, since he sat down on the edge and swung his legs over. I was still lying on my side, with my head pillowed on my folded arm.

"So you had questions for me. Shoot." He flicked at my nose again with his finger and lay down so that our eyes were level.

I toyed with a loose thread on the coverlet. "Everything you know...about sex. What we did. You've been with a lot of girls, haven't you?"

He didn't waver. "I've been with a few. But most of what I know came from when I was dating my high school girlfriend. We were both virgins until we were sixteen, and so we learned everything together. My aunt is pretty cool, too. When she suspected that Laurie and I were sleeping together, she gave me a book that was about other stuff than just being safe and waiting for marriage. That's where I found out more about the female anatomy than most guys ever know." He winked at me. "Laurie was happy about that."

"I can't complain, either." I leaned to kiss the side of his jaw and let my fingers skitter across the scruff of beard on his cheek. "Do you think I'm weird because I waited until James and I got married?"

"Absolutely not." Tom skimmed his hand down my arm. "I think it's a good choice. But James is an asshole who didn't know how to make love to his own wife, and didn't care enough to find out. That's not on you, sweetheart. I'm willing to bet he wasn't a virgin. And even if he was, he's the man. It was his job to take care of you."

I nodded. "Okay. I have another question. You don't have to answer it." I took a deep breath. "Why did you have condoms with you tonight? Did you plan to find a girl to sleep with?" My unspoken addition hung between us. *Was I just convenient?*

He picked up a strand of my hair and twisted it around his finger. "No, what happened tonight wasn't part of any plan. The Army issues condoms to every soldier. I always keep them in my bag. That's why I had them." He slid his hand through my hair to cradle my head. "When I decided to take the bus to the shore, I only thought I might sleep in a real bed, eat dinner at a nice restaurant and maybe go on some of the amusements on the boardwalk. That was it."

A smile curved my lips. "Well, you know, it's Saturday night. The rides are open late. We can get dressed and go over there if you feel like you might be missing something. . ." I pushed myself to sit up, moving as though I were climbing out of bed.

Tom grabbed me around the waist, and I shrieked as he pulled me back. "The only amusement I want tonight is right here in front of me." He guided my head down and held me in place as his lips teased against mine.

After my last climax, I'd thought there was no way I could want him again tonight. I was thoroughly sated. But as his tongue made forays into my mouth and his hand dropped to cover my breast, that idea drifted away.

He released my head, and I sat up, staring down into blue eyes that were suddenly clouded. I traced the lines of his face, memorizing each angle and texture. A lump rose in my throat as I considered that in all probability, I would never touch this man again after tonight. Earlier, when we'd sat in the driveway and I'd asked him to stay with me, the notion that we'd never see each other again had been wild and daring, an assurance that I could be whoever I wanted tonight, with no repercussions. No consequences. Now, it felt horribly wrong, wrenching and painful.

"Caroline." Tom held my face between his hands and brushed my cheekbones with his thumbs, as though wiping away tears that I knew had not yet fallen. He seemed about to say something else, and then he shook his head. "Will you dance with me?"

"Dance?" I furrowed my brow. "To what music?"

"I saw a radio in the kitchen. Come on. If I only have one night with you, I want it all." He stood up and pulled me to my feet.

"Are we dancing naked?" Not that I was opposed to the idea, but I had never considered such a thing.

"Of course not." Tom grinned at me, and in that moment, I think I fell a little bit in love with him. He picked up his boxers and stepped into them, and then snagged his uniform shirt from the back of the chair. "Put your arms out."

I obeyed, and he slipped one sleeve and then the other over my arms. It hung down to mid-thigh, and he buttoned it with great care.

"There we go. Now we're proper." He held my hand and led me to the dark kitchen. I leaned against the counter as he fumbled with the ancient radio, his eyes narrowed in concentration as he tried to tune in a decent song.

"No surf music." I stuck out my tongue. "I hate that stuff."

He turned to look at me, mouth open in shock and a hand over his heart. "Sweetheart, you're killing me. I'm a California boy, remember. The surfing is in our blood."

"So do it, but don't sing about."

He sighed and shook his head. "Okay, so no Beach Boys. How about the Brits? Are you against them, too?"

I shrugged. "Some of them are okay. Herman's Hermits are good."

"Hmmm. I think you need some lessons in musical taste."

I stepped forward to wrap my arms around his waist. "Are those lessons as much fun as tonight's have been?"

He glanced at me over his shoulder, one eyebrow raised. "Behave yourself. Music is serious business." He twisted the knob, and a familiar voice filled the kitchen.

"Mel Carter. Does he meet your strict requirements?" Tom held out a hand to me.

"He sings a hell of a love song." I let him pull me close, and we began swaying together, letting Mel's words wash over us. My head rested on Tom's chest, my ear against his heart. I circled his waist with my arms, and he let his hands dangle together at my lower back.

Kiss me, kiss me, when you do I know that you will miss me. . .

Standing so close to him in the dark room, letting our feet move in a small circle on the cold linoleum floor, it would've been easy to let my imagination run. I might have pictured summers in the future, warm days when we would have all the time in the world to get to know each other, to find out about our likes and tastes. I might have dreamed of playing in the sand with small children who had vivid blue eyes and my blonde hair. I could've imagined a time when this night would've been only the beginning of a life together, not a matter of hours snatched when our worlds collided.

If I'd let my mind wander down those paths, I would've sobbed into his bare chest at the injustice of a life where I'd wasted too many years on a sham of a relationship and where the one man I might have loved forever was crossing the ocean to fight for a country I couldn't even find on the map.

But I didn't. I concentrated on the movement of our feet together, on the tickle of his fingers grazing my back, on the feel of his skin beneath my cheek. For those moments, neither the future nor the past existed for us.

When the song died out, Jackie DeShannon began to sing about what the world needed now. We kept moving, neither of us willing to break the spell.

"There's so much more I want to show you, and not enough time." The rumble of Tom's voice startled my eyes open.

"We have tonight. We won't waste it thinking about what we'd do if things were different." I stepped back to look up at him. "Tell me, though. If tonight were endless, what would you teach me? What else would we do?"

He understood me, and he didn't bring up anything that we could do outside the house. "The bathtub. I'd run us a bubble bath, and I'd wash you, and you'd wash me, and probably half the water would end up sloshing out onto the floor."

I smiled at the idea. "I like that one. What else?"

"Hmmm." He cast his eyes up toward the ceiling as though considering about his answer. While he thought, we wandered into the living room, and Tom sat on the sofa, folding me onto his lap.

"So many different positions. We'd try them all, and you could tell me which ones were your favorites."

"Positions? There's other ways to do it?"

Tom laughed and pulled my face to his. "Oh, my sweet innocent, what I wouldn't give for all the time in the world to show you." He smoothed my hair away from my face, and his eyes sobered. "Promise me, Caroline, that you'll find someone. Some good guy who'll treat you well and be the man you need. Don't spend any more time being lonely, okay?" He attempted a smile. "After all the effort I've put into teaching you, it would be a shame to let it go to waste."

I wanted to scream that I didn't want another man touching me, but instead I changed the subject. "Tell me what else we'd do."

"Well, location, location, location. I'd take you in every bed, right here on this sofa, up on the kitchen counters. . ."

"The counters?" I made a face. "I don't know how that would work."

"Trust me, it would. The height's just about perfect."

We sat in the dark, listening to the music, while Tom stroked my hair and I listened to his heart. I fought against drowsiness, even though I knew it had to be well after midnight. I didn't want to waste a second of our time together.

"Caroline." He whispered my name, as though there were anyone nearby to be bothered if he spoke aloud.

"Hmmm?" I snuggled closer to him, drawing my feet up to rest on his leg.

"Once more. Let me take you back to bed, and we'll be together once more."

I rose up on my knees and straddled him, forcing a smile that I was sure didn't reach my eyes. "Yes, please."

Tilting my head, I kissed him, just the softest touch of lips to lips, as his hands delved beneath the shirt I wore to cup my breasts and tease my nipples to stiffness. He moved one hand to my back and pushed me forward until his mouth covered one nipple, laving it through the cotton of the shirt. I arched my back and held his head in place, feeling strong and sensual again.

"I'll never look at this uniform blouse the same way again." Tom grinned as he moved to the other side to pay the same attention to my other nipple. "I'll probably get hard every time I put it on, thinking about you in it."

I laughed softly. "I hope you do. But that'd be awkward, wouldn't it?"

"Yeah, it would be difficult to explain." He slid his hands around to lift me until my core, already wet and ready, was centered over his cock, once again stretching the boxers. I wriggled and he hissed.

"If you keep that up, we're not going to make it to the bedroom." He stood up, bringing me with him, shifting to hold me by the ass. I kissed up and down his neck as we walked, nipping at the warm skin until he laid me across the bed.

"I know I wanted you to learn how to say what you want. I think you got that part down. This time, I don't want you to say anything. Show me what you want, without speaking. I'll do the same. But we'll both stay completely silent." He stopped at the chair to fish another condom out of the pocket of his pants.

"You don't have to use that. I told you, I'm on the pill." I rolled to the middle of the bed, waiting for him.

"I know. But I can't take any chances, baby. I have to do everything I can to keep you safe." He sat down and began unbuttoning his shirt, still on me. "Believe me. . . .under different circumstances, in another life, knowing you were carrying my child would be. . . ." He shook his head. "Beyond words. But I can't risk doing that to you when I'm leaving to go overseas."

He undid the last button and lifted me up to take off the shirt. For a few beats of my heart, his eyes roamed over my body, hungry and wanting. When he stood, he shucked off the boxers and climbed over to lie down next to me.

"You're in control, Caroline. Show me. What do you want?"

The answer to that question was so involved that I couldn't begin to know it. I lay still, my eyes closed, taking inventory of my body and where I wanted to be touched. Pressing down onto the mattress, I rose to sit on my knees, the bottoms of my feet flat against my butt. Tom watched me, waiting.

I lifted his hand from bed, holding it between both of mine. I flashed back to seeing these fingers on the steering wheel of my car earlier, wanting them to touch me even then. Sealing my palm against his, I knit our fingers together and brought his knuckles to my lips. I pressed open-mouthed kisses to each one, letting my tongue drift out and delve into the valleys between the bones. Tom's eyes drifted closed, and his breathing picked up.

Pulling my hand away from his, I turned the palm up and kissed it before I lowered it to cover my breast. I centered his hand so that my nipple was in the middle of his palm, moving it slowly as the pink bud stiffened. His fingers closed on it, rolling the peak. He slid his hand below to palm me, lifting the weight as his thumb continued to rub my nipple into an aching point.

I bit down on my lip to hold back a moan. His talented fingers were driving me mad, and I was sure that even with his eyes closed, he could tell by the way my chest was heaving. His other hand joined in, teasing the rosy crests until I couldn't sit still.

As though sensing it, Tom lowered his hands to grasp my hips and guide me closer, lifting one leg over his abdomen so that I straddled his middle. I could feel his cock along my back, but I didn't have the chance to touch him before he shifted me so that his lips could reach my tits. He focused all of his attention on one at a time, sucking the nipple into his mouth and tugging at it as his tongue licked and stroked. I closed my eyes, just letting myself feel every sensation.

His hand circled my wrist and brought my hand up, flattening it against my other breast. My eyes flew open, and I looked down at him with wide, questioning eyes. He nodded at me, the edges of his mouth curling into a smile as he moved my hand for me, his gaze like molten lava pouring over me. My tongue darted out to wet my lips, and then I rubbed at my own nipple, experimenting to see what felt best. Tom's eyes darkened as he watched me.

I'd never made any noise during what had passed for sex, so it was strange that I was having such a tough time keeping quiet now. I gritted my teeth against the groans that wanted to escape my throat. But it heightened every pleasure as well.

Tom released my nipple with one last lap of his tongue. His hands wandered up my thighs and tantalized nearly to the juncture of my legs. He reached for my other hand as it rested on my knee, and this time, he brought it to the one spot I needed him to touch me. Holding my fingers with his own, he dipped them into the wet folds, moving up and down.

I wanted to tell him that I couldn't do this, couldn't touch myself while he watched me, but he'd made me promise not to speak. He nudged my hand in encouragement, and I swallowed hard before doing as he asked.

My pussy was slick and slippery under my fingertips. I tried to mimic the way he had touched me earlier, finding the hard sensitive knob at the top and then sliding down to my entrance. It was an entirely different feeling from Tom's touch, but I could tell he approved by the way his breathing picked up, his chest moving up and down rapidly as his lips parted.

I began stroking myself faster, harder. Tom's eyes closed and his mouth snapped shut, his clenched jaw telling me that keeping silent wasn't any easier on him than it was on me. Abruptly he gripped my waist to hold me still as he rolled to retrieve the condom from the nightstand.

Sitting up, he eased me backward, lifting me onto his outstretched legs so that his pulsing erection sat between us. The rip of the condom wrapper was the only sound beyond our pounding hearts and panting breaths. As he began to put the rubber on, I held his hand, stilling it.

Tom frowned at me, and I knew he was thinking of what I'd said earlier about not needing it. I shook my head, smiling and took the condom from him, rolling it down over his heated flesh.

I thought he would flip us over and enter me that way, but instead, he nudged me to rise up on my knees. His fingers delved into my wet folds, rubbing my clit until my world shrunk to only his hands on me. He guided me over his cock and raised his hips to impale me.

This position was radically different from being under him. Tom lifted me up a little, and I understood he wanted me to find my own rhythm here. I gasped, loving the drag of his huge member on the inside of my pussy. One of my own hands drifted up to pinch my nipple, and Tom slid his fingers between my legs again.

I felt alive, wild and free for the first time in my life. I threw back my head and opened my mouth, sucking in breath as fast as I could. Tom began to buck up against me faster, driving us both up and over the edge. I came hard, unable to hold back the cry as my inner channels gripped at his cock. His body stiffened into one singular hard muscle, and he growled out my name, his fingers death-gripping my thighs.

I melted onto his chest, smiling at the sound of his pounding heart beneath my ear. His arms wrapped around me as one hand caressed my ass.

"You cheated." My voice was muffled against his skin. "I heard you at the end."

Tom shook with laughter. "I wasn't the only one, sweetheart. Still, you were amazing. I thought for sure you were going to give up and say something at one point, but you didn't. That was...wow." He brushed my hair out of my face, and I felt his lips on the top of my head.

It was that simple action that broke me. Tears that I couldn't fight anymore flooded my eyes and ran down my cheeks, splashing onto Tom's chest. I shook with sobs that I didn't want him to feel.

"Baby." I heard the desperation in his voice. "Caroline. Please don't cry. I'm sorry."

"Why are you sorry?" I swiped angrily at my face. "You haven't done anything to be sorry about."

"I'm sorry that you're crying. I'm sorry that I can't stay with you. I'm sorry that I have to leave. I'm sorry..." He broke a little. "Sorry if you regret tonight."

I pushed up on my arms, staring down at his tormented eyes. "Never. Not one bit. This was the best night of my life, Tom. If I die tomorrow, I'll at least know I've lived, not just existed. You gave me that. I'll never forget it. I'll never forget you."

He pulled me back down to his chest, tucking me under his chin. I couldn't stop crying, but I didn't care anymore. He held me as I sobbed, stroking my back and my head, but not speaking until I had quieted.

"Caroline, you may not realize it, but you gave me an incredible gift tonight, too. I'll never forget you, either."

I twisted so that I could see the side of his face. "I'll write to you. Just give me the address, and I promise, every day—"

But he only shook his head. "No. Not because I don't want you to, because, God, more than anything, I do. But I'm going to be so far away for so long, baby. And you're going to be here, starting to live your life again, like you promised me. Pretty soon, or maybe not that soon, but one day, you're going to meet someone, a guy who appreciates you and treats you like you deserve. Then tonight won't be anything but a memory, something that happened to a girl you hardly remember. You'll want to stop writing, but you'll feel guilty, and I can't take that."

New tears leaked from my eyes. "Never. I'll wait for you, I promise."

He sighed, long and deep. "I know you would. But I can't ask that of you. And from my side, I have to get through this. Caroline, I'm scared. I've lived through shit before, I've seen death, but I'm not afraid to tell you the idea of going over there and fighting frightens the hell out of me. I need to be blinders-on, put my head down and bull through. If I'm thinking about you, waiting for letters, I could get careless. So. . .no. This. . .tonight. . .like you said before, it's all we have. It has to be enough."

I sniffled. Part of me wanted to argue with him, rail against his stupid logic, but another part wouldn't let me waste our time together like that. Instead, I drew in a shuddering breath.

"If you weren't in the Army, if you weren't going away, would you want to see me again?" I wasn't sure I wanted to hear the answer.

Tom held my shoulders and raised me until he could look into my eyes. "Yes. Absolutely, a hundred percent yes. If I didn't have this fucking commitment, we'd wake up together tomorrow morning, and I swear, Caroline, I'd haul your sweet ass down to the courthouse and marry you. And then I'd take you on the honeymoon of your dreams, all over the world, and we'd make love in a new bed every night."

I smiled, settling back on top of him and letting my eyes close. "Tell me more. Tell me what would happen next."

His voice softened, and he rubbed my back as he spoke. "After a year-long honeymoon, I'd take you back to California with me, and then you could go to law school. I'd go back to work—"

"What did you do before the Army, anyway?" I hadn't even asked him that.

He hesitated. "I own a publishing company. My parents left it to me. I was working my way up the ranks, though, so I'd be qualified to run it someday. My aunt insisted on that."

"I think I'd like your aunt."

"Ha!" He chuckled. "My aunt would love you. She'd probably want you to come work for her. And maybe you would, for a few years, until the babies come along."

"Babies?" Sleep was chasing me, but I managed to ask that one question.

"Of course. Beautiful blonde-haired babies, pretty and smart as their mom. I think we'd have a girl first, and then a boy, and we'd buy a house right on the beach so they could both learn to surf. And every night, you and I would take a long walk together on the beach, and we'd tell each other about our day. Then after the kids were in bed, I'd make love to you over and over, so you'd never forget how beautiful and sexy you are, and how much I love you. . ."

The closing of a door awoke me with a start. I sat up in bed and glanced around the still-dark room, disoriented. It took a few minutes before I remembered that I was at Aunt Susan's house, at the shore. And then everything came flooding back over me.

Tom.

I panicked, realizing he wasn't in the room with me. Had he really left without telling me good-bye? And then I spotted his duffel bag, propped against the edge of the door. I fell back onto the pillows, and suddenly, as an idea occurred to me, I rolled over and pulled open the nightstand drawer, blessing my dependable aunt who always kept paper and pens there.

Moments later, I heard the bathroom door open and Tom's steps in the hallway. I curled onto my side with my hand tucked under my face, the sheet pulled up above my breasts.

He stopped in the doorway, and for a minute, he only looked down at me, not saying a word. When he moved toward the bed, I scooted over to make room. He was dressed in his uniform again, looking every bit the handsome solider I'd met the day before. He'd shaved, and I ventured a finger up to stroke his smooth cheek. He caught my hand and wove our fingers together.

"Hi." Tom leaned down to kiss my cheek. "Are you okay?"

I nodded, unable to trust myself to speak yet.

"All right. Good. I found the phone book, and I called a taxi to take me to the bus station. It should be here any minute."

My throat swelled shut as panic gripped me. *No.* He couldn't leave me. Not like this, not now.

I struggled to swallow. "I could drive you back to post. I have the car, and it's not like I have anything to do here. It would be faster than taking the bus, and nicer, and we could have those extra hours. . ."

But he was shaking his head even as I spoke. "No, baby. God, I want to say yes, but if I do, I'll never be able to let you go. I want to remember you here, lying naked in bed, all tousled and sleepy and warm. Let me have that."

I nodded, knowing he was right. If I drove down to Fort Dix, I might never leave. I might stay there, camped outside the gates, just waiting to catch one last glimpse.

"Caroline, there's so much I want to say, and so much I shouldn't. I don't have time to do it justice. So just let me kiss you once more, and then you roll over and close your eyes."

I pushed myself to sit up, letting the sheet flutter around my waist. Tom held my face in his hands as though I were something precious and fragile. He closed his eyes as his lips covered mine in a slow, sweet kiss. I opened my mouth, inviting his tongue to dance with mine one more time.

I would have sat there for an eternity, my lips melted to his, but Tom drew back, his eyes dark. He ran his hand down my hair one more time.

"Good-bye, Caroline."

He stood up, turned around and picked up his duffel bag. Without a single glance back, he walked out of the room and down the hall. I heard the squeak of the front door, and then the definitive click as it shut behind him.

Time froze for the space of ten seconds. My heart stopped beating, I didn't breathe, and I didn't move.

And then I heard the sound of a car pulling away, and there was only silence.

The 6:10 bus from Ocean City to Jackson via Lakewood was on time for once. The driver nodded to the regulars and to the vacationers who'd taken a day at the beach and now were heading back to real life. At the end of the line of boarding passengers, he spied a soldier in khaki, a duffel bag flung over his shoulder.

Brought him back to the old days, that sight did. He'd been a youngster when he started driving twenty years before, and in those days, it was a rare day he didn't have a soldier or a sailor on his bus. Getting to be more common again now. He shook his head. The more times change. . .

This young man climbed onto the bus, handed in his ticket and moved to the back without speaking. He dropped his bag onto an empty seat and then sank down next to the window. He knew he should sleep, but instead he kept his eyes fastened on the window, where the first pink rays of sunlight were beginning to light the sky, driving away the dark. He didn't move as the doors closed and the rig rumbled out of the station and onto the road.

They'd been driving for a solid thirty minutes when he finally shifted in his seat, looking away from the passing scenery. He was restless and angry and despondent and scared. He ran a hand over the stubble on the top of his head and remembered the paperback mystery he'd tucked into his bag before he'd left Fort Dix. Anything to take his mind off last night. Off. . .her.

He unfastened the bag and tilted it so that he could see inside, sliding his hand to reach for the book. When his fingers touched paper, he frowned and pulled it out.

It was a single sheet of thin white stationary, folded once. Tom opened it and looked at the unfamiliar script.

In case you change your mind. Because. . .I think we could have it all.

Below, in the same firm hand, was her name and address. Tom's breath caught. She'd put the ball firmly in his court. What he chose to do with this information was completely his decision. She'd taken a risk, doing this; he knew that even if she convinced herself otherwise, for weeks or even months, she'd wonder and hope each time the mail arrived.

He knew what he should do. He should crumble this note and drop it into the trash can when they changed buses at Lakeview. He should forget it, and her. It was the kindest thing for both of them.

He sat staring down at it for a long time. And then he dug into his bag again, this time pulling out a pad of paper and pen.

Dear Caroline...

Caroline and Tom's story continues in
Baby, I'm Yours
Good Vibrations Book #2
(February, 2016)
and
Save It For Me
Good Vibrations Book #3
(Releasing June, 2016)

More Than Words
Play List

More Than Words—Extreme
Mrs. Brown, You've Got a Lovely Daughter-Herman's Hermits
Stop! In the Name of Love—The Supremes
What the World Needs Now is Love—Jackie DeShannon
Hold Me, Thrill Me, Kiss Me—Mel Carter

About Emma

Emma Fallon is a southern girl with a penchant for long nights under the stars with hot men. She writes and reads erotic romance and has a special weakness for historical erotica. She can be enticed to do just about anything. . .as long as there's chocolate involved.

Follow her on Facebook and Twitter . . . keep up with her releases on her website (http://emmadfallon.com) . . .
. . .and finally, subscribe to her special events newsletter (http://tiny.cc/EmmaNewsletter) so you don't miss any fun.

Oh, and be sure to check out Emma's biggest fans, the Naughty Temptresses, on Facebook!

More from Emma

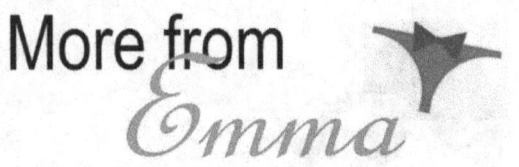

The Small Town Swingers Serial

Welcome to Paradise
The Heat Is On
Night Moves
Fading Into You

Good Vibrations Series

More Than Words
Baby, I'm Yours
Save It For Me